This Book Belongs to:

_____

DESTINY IMAGE® PUBLISHERS, INC.
P.O. Box 310, Shippensburg, PA 17257-0310
"Promoting Inspired Lives."

Illustrations by R.W. Lamont Hunt

This book and all other Destiny Image and Destiny Image Fiction books are available at Christian bookstores and distributors worldwide.

For more information on foreign distributors, call 717-532-3040.
Or reach us on the Internet: www.destinyimage.com

ISBN 13: 978-0-7684-1584-1
ISBN 13 EBook: 978-0-7684-1585-8

For Worldwide Distribution, Printed in the U.S.A.
1 2 3 4 5 6 7 8 9 10 11 / 22 21 20 19 18 17

GOD
IS REALLY
GOOD

BILL JOHNSON
WITH SETH DAHL

ILLUSTRATED BY R.W. LAMONT HUNT

Sparrow wakes up in his nest
and stretches his wings.

Dad has just
returned from
finding his
favorite
breakfast—
worm cereal!

4

Sparrow and Mom and Dad say prayers and eat their meal.

When Sparrow finishes, he hugs Mom before flying off to see his friends.

"Remember, stay in our forest," Mom chirps as he flies away.

5

Sparrow flies toward Squirrel's house
and lands on a nearby branch.

When Squirrel comes out,
Sparrow notices she is a
little worried.

"I'm running out of acorns,"
Squirrel moans.

6

"And I'm not sure I will find any more before winter.

"I'll have to start looking in another forest."

"Oh no!" says Sparrow.
"What will you do? I want
to help, but Mom says I
can't leave the forest."

"Thank you,"
says Squirrel.

"It's kind of you
to offer to help. But
don't look so worried.
God is good."

8

Sparrow can't help but worry anyway. Squirrel needs
acorns to eat during the winter
and he wants to help.

He heads off toward
Owl's house.

"Owl is wise,"
Sparrow thinks to
himself, "he will know
what to do."

Owl hears someone land on his branch.
"Good morning,"
Owl calls out.

"Owl!" says Sparrow.
"Squirrel is running out of
acorns! What will we do?"

"Hmm,"
Owl replies.

"That is a
problem.

"Perhaps she should
look in another
forest."

"Can you help her?" Sparrow asks Owl.

"I wish I could," Owl
replies. "But my eyesight isn't
very good anymore. I can't
see something as small
as an acorn."

"Oh, no!" Sparrow says.
"Oh, Sparrow," says Owl. "Please don't worry.
God is good."

11

But Sparrow can't help worrying.

Every day is one day closer to winter. And no one could help Squirrel.

What would they do?

12

"This is not good," Sparrow thinks again as he flies off to see his friend, Puppy.

"Puppy has a good nose.

"Maybe she can sniff the acorns out."

13

Sparrow lands on the doghouse, and Puppy walks out.
"Hello, Sparrow," she says.

"Hi Puppy! Squirrel is running out of acorns and needs
help finding more."

"Can you use your
nose to help find
some?" Sparrow asks.

"I wish I could help,"
says Puppy.

"But my family keeps me fenced in the yard. I'm sorry, but there's no way I can get out to help find acorns."

"This is not good," Sparrow murmurs to himself. "What will we do?"

"I'm sure Squirrel will find some acorns," says Puppy encouragingly.

"Don't worry, God is good."

15

Sparrow barely hears Puppy as
he heads toward the field.

"Goat will help! Goat can jump the
fence and go anywhere," he says to
himself as he lands.

16

Sparrow tells Goat all about Squirrel's problems, and how no one else can help.

"I want to help, Sparrow, but I'm too afraid," says Goat.

HHOOooWWWWWLLL HHOOooWWWWWLLL HHOooWWWWWLLL

"What are you afraid of?" asks Sparrow.

"Coyotes. All night long I hear them howling over the hill. If I left my field, it would be too dangerous!" says Goat.

17

As Sparrow listens to Goat, he too begins to feel afraid in the forest. It no longer feels like the safe place it was this morning.

Every shadow seems darker and every sound makes him jump.

Suddenly, Cat jumps out of the bushes, startling Sparrow into racing away as quickly as he can.

He's too scared to hear her shout, "Sorry, Sparrow!"

19

As he catches his breath, Sparrow thinks over all he's realized today.

When he left his nest this morning, he felt good, but now he is worried about all the problems his friends were having in the forest.

He then realizes he's flying
over the fence surrounding
Lily's garden, so he lands
on a post to talk to her.

21

"Sparrow, I haven't heard your song all day,"
Lily says as Sparrow lands.
"Are you okay?"

"Oh Lily,"
Sparrow says, "I
can't sing today.

There are so many
things that are
not good."

22

Sparrow tells Lily all that's happening. About Squirrel not having enough acorns.

About Owl not seeing well, and Puppy being penned up.

How Goat is afraid of the coyotes at night, and how Cat scared him.

"Everyone keeps saying God is good and takes care of all of us," he says, "but I'm not so sure anymore."

23

To his surprise, Lily is still cheerful after hearing all that's going on. She then tells Sparrow about her day. "God is really good to me," she begins. "He gave me the sun, and I've been reaching toward it all morning."

"But there's no rain today, Lily. Aren't you thirsty?" asks Sparrow. "Aren't you worried you won't be able to keep growing?"

"Oh no," says Lily, "When there's no rain, the family that lives here pours water on me. I always have enough."

"What about when it storms and the wind blows? The days you can't see the sun?" says Sparrow.

"Those days are the most important," replies Lily. "Without them, I wouldn't push my roots further into the soil. Those days make me so strong.

"Even when it seems like I'm having
a hard time, God's making
me stronger."

"So God is really good to you, Lily, but is
He really good to all of us?
What about Squirrel, and Owl, and Puppy
and Goat?" says Sparrow.

26

"Oh Sparrow, God
is really good to you
and to your friends. You're
having a tough time seeing it
because you are so focused on
everything you think
is not good,"
Lily explains.

27

Lily smiles. "If you want to fly, you must first let go of the fence, right?"

"Yes, but what does flying have to do with my worries?"
Sparrow asks.

"It has everything to do with it, Sparrow. You are holding onto things that are not good, just like you are holding onto this fence.

"God didn't create you for this, He created you to fly, but you have to let it all go first."

29

"But even if I fly, I still can't help
Squirrel or Owl or Puppy or Goat,"
Sparrow says.

"Oh Sparrow," says Lily.
"This is just a time when God
is making them stronger.

"Like the rain on
my roots.

"And Owl has trouble seeing things, but his grandchildren come to help him every day. He's growing closer to them with each visit.

"And Puppy may be penned up, but her family takes her for walks every day, and they only keep her in the yard to protect her from harm.

"And though Goat is afraid of the wilderness, he knows his field is safe from anything that might hurt him."

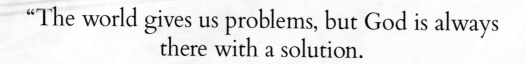

"The world gives us problems, but God is always there with a solution.

"Like Squirrel. You said she doesn't have enough acorns right now. That's a problem the world has given her. But God is always working to help us even when we don't see it.

"Tell me, Sparrow, what kind of tree does Squirrel live in?"

Sparrow thinks for a moment.
"She lives in a big oak tree."

Lily smiles. "There you have it! Acorns come from oak trees.

"When
Autumn comes,
Squirrel will have
more acorns
than she can eat.
Isn't God good?"

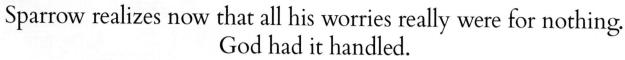

Sparrow realizes now that all his worries really were for nothing. God had it handled.

"You're right, Lily! God is really good to us!" Sparrow says. "Thank you!"

At that moment, Sparrow lets go of the fence, and he also lets go of all the worries he'd been holding on to.

He rockets up into the air with a
happy song.

The world still has its problems,
but Sparrow can be sure…

God is Really Good!

The End.

BILL JOHNSON

Bill Johnson is a fifth-generation pastor with a rich heritage in the Holy Spirit. Bill and his wife, Beni, are the senior leaders of Bethel Church in Redding, California, and serve a growing number of churches that cross denominational lines, demonstrate power, and partner for revival. Bill's vision is for all believers to experience God's presence and operate in the miraculous—as expressed in his bestselling books *When Heaven Invades Earth* and *Hosting the Presence*. The Johnsons have three children and nine grandchildren.

SETH DAHL

Seth Dahl is the Children's Pastor at Bethel Church in Redding, California. His passion is to bring God's Kingdom with signs and wonders, connecting children to the Father's heart so they will serve Him all the days of their lives. Seth and his wife, Lauren, live on a small farm with their three children.

LAMONT HUNT

Lamont Hunt is an award winning character animator and illustrator, currently bouncing back and forth between Los Angeles and Sioux Falls, South Dakota. He has won several awards for his work in short films. He was also a character animator on the 2017 film "The Nut Job 2." Previously, Lamont illustrated Shawn Bolz's *Growing Up With God*. Contact him at www. dakotakidcreations.com.